BLOOD ORCHID

TYESHA J. FRANKLIN

Onyx has always been a runner.

Every time period, every moment in history.

Running.

The past lives that she has lived have kept her happy and fulfilled that is until he shows up. He has begun following her trail since she became a runner but now she must face the facts….

She won't be able to run forever.

Running helps her becoming free.

Fighting back will make her a survivor.

Dedication

This novel is dedicated to my grandpa, John Gilbert, who never stopped believing in me and my creative mind.

I would also like to dedicate this novel to my Uncle Rufus..., who gave me the first computer I ever used and how he always motivated me to work hard towards my dream.

"A lie that is half-truth is the darkest of all lies."
ALFRED TENNYSON

Tango of Saints and Sinners

A deadly game is played and no one ever wins.
the music withers away like a black rose on its last petal.
he stabs the newcomer to keep what is rightfully mended.

tears are never shed; lights begin to dim;
she leaves the stage without a partner;
tired of the dance between saints and sins.

Prologue

Death by Sight

LIGHT ESCAPED HIS GRASP AS he trotted through the unfamiliar forest. He had never been through as much pain as he had been a victim to nor had he witnessed in such a horrid place. Every night he heard screaming and morning he saw bodies being thrown away like garbage. The torture and torment seemed to have lasted a lifetime, even though it may have been only a few days. Maybe weeks. Time slipped by every passing second he stayed in that madhouse. How he had managed to escape from them was beyond him. The only thing that mattered now was that he was free. And as he began to trench through the dark parts of the woodlands, he realized this was the first time he had smiled in a very long time. *I'm free, I can go back home…home.* The thought made Jamie's heart flutter with excitement. He wondered if anything had changed since he had been gone, since he had been taken from everything he knew and loved. He sighed with utter defeat; Jamie knew he would never be safe as long as he was alive. He could never go home.

It never dawned on Jamie that so much of his life had been toyed with, but he realized that the game would soon be over. He's life was meaningless. The only question that remained was: would he be able to survive the deadly game of prey and predator? As Jamie made his way through the trenches, he began to lose his breath and consciousness.

Maybe because of the malnutrition he suffered from, or the blood loss from the countless beatings and bloodlettings, but with each passing moment his condition began to worsen. Whatever the reason, he knew his chance for survival was fleeting.

It was too late to think about his mistakes or regrets because he knew that, even with the last few moments of his life, he could not trust anyone. The chilled wind pushed him faster against time, against his enemy. Thinking about who might be coming for him made Jamie pick up his pace. As he ran through the forest, the thought of someone following him petrified his imagination.

"Why me," he screamed inside of his mind. *Because no one leaves.* Pushing himself closer to the edge, Jamie found that even with the ability to escape, he would never have the strength and menace to fight back. *No one ever escapes alive.* Before he could reach the end of the cliff, a deadly force slammed into his chest, causing him to forcefully collide into a solid oak tree. His brown eyes were overlapping with the dilation of his pupils. His black hair was plastered over his face with both blood and sweat. There was no escape. He would die tonight.

"What do you want with me," he screamed as thunder boomed throughout the trees, but only the dead silence and whisper of the wind answered him.

"Just get it over with, I'm ready to die! You have nothing left to use against me. So just end it already," Jamie cried as he hopelessly fell to his knees. His sobs and screams pushed the limbs and branches of the nearby trees. As Jamie scanned the area he saw nothing, but was too frightened to try and run away again. Even if he could run, the thought of the pain from being slammed into the trees almost made Jamie vomit.

'Broken rib cage,' a voice whispered in his mind. CRACK! He screeched as he tried to push the bones back into place. SNAP, a foot slammed down on his femur.

"Please stop," Jamie tearfully slobbered as the pain began to echo and ring though his ears. Blood began to slither out the corner of his mouth as he coughed and seized in pain and agony. "I'm begging you, please don't do this," he pleaded. His vision began to blur as the blood collided with the rain. A shadow appeared in front of him as lightning guided the rain to the ground. Shrouded in fog and darkness, the figure pushed Jamie's head against the trunk of the tree.

When Jamie saw his attacker, he could not help but laugh. "You— you bastard, how could you! How could you do this to me? I thought I could trust you! If they find out, you are dead. Do you hear me, you traitorous monster, you are dead." SNAP, the stranger's foot began to crush his windpipe as he tried to speak. Jamie's teeth began to grind and crack against the surface and roof of his mouth to the result that many of his teeth were cracking and falling from his face. Some of them even slid down his throat. He nudged his body away from the figure long enough to slither away to the dead tree trunk. It seemed that everything in the forest was either dead or dying, and soon Jamie would follow suit. Even with the little strength that he had left, Jamie knew that it did not matter: his life would soon be over.

"I swore I would not tell a soul, not even you. I won't talk. They trusted me with the truth. KILL ME! Kill me but I swear you will not get me to say a word. I will stay loyal unlike you—so get it over will. Finish me off and be done with it! Just do it already; it's what you've wanted to do for so long. So get it over with, you bastard. Go on, that's what you really want, so finish it!'

And without hesitation, the stranger yanked back Jamie's head and twisted the tip of his spinal cord out of his body.

Everything had been taken care of. All that was left was to destroy what was left of the coward. The figure gathered the limp and feeble corpse to the nearest lifeless oak trunk. Snatching and pulling away limbs and branches from growing trees would help hide the remains. People would see the sight as nothing but a freak act of nature destroying what was left of the surroundings. The dead leaves and branches would make the fire burn quicker, before the sun would rise. One spark was all that was needed.

Slowly the smoke began to rise and swarm the sky. The corpse began to ignite against the fire and Jamie's lifeless eyes stared back at his murderer. Watching but seeing nothing-the flames began to flicker, grow and eat away at everything that surrounded the body. As the figure fed the fire more and more of the dying earth, he felt water fall against his face. He smiled harder knowing the rain would finish the rest of the job before anyone would come to explore the usual smoke in the area. Yellow and orange lights danced against the droplets of rain and disappeared into the puddles. As the smolder began to clear, nothing was left but two shiny plates that refused to burn. The murderer picked up the necklace and transferred it from one knuckle to the other until it was against the thumb. Without hesitation, the figure flung the dog tag into the nearby trench. There was no trace left of Jamie. He was dead and finally free.

You got what you wanted—to take that secret to the grave,' black eyes flickered against the fire as the rain began to settle. 'I hope your loyal for her was worth dying for. And if not you'll see each other again.'

Chapter One

Unquenched

It did not seem like a big deal to her. Sitting in a class where she knew the information, and Onyx was sure she probably knew more than the teacher himself. One of the few classes that she did not care about because she had first handed knowledge about the subject in discussion. She could have just as easily skipped class, arrived on any given test day and pass the subject with the highest marks in the class. But then she would have to find a way to entertain herself for an hour and a half before her next class and she really enjoyed watching her teacher make himself miserable.

Mr. Rocnard, a poor misshapen stubby little fellow that could hardly form a complete sentence let alone give an entire seminar on different time periods in history. Rocnard began to stumble across every line in the textbook, not that she was paying attention to him. His dull and hoarse voice made a short impression on her from the moment he introduce himself to the class at the beginning of the term. Onyx let her mind wonder to different aspects that were never related to history class let alone high school for that matter. She stared out of the window waiting for the day to end. Until the scent started to fill the air. As the teacher shrugged off his black coat she had to snicker to herself. The stains under his arms and on his back could have led anyone to think that it was too hot inside the small classroom. She zeroed in on the air conditioning and saw it was sixty-five degrees inside. The sun scorched and burned outside at ninety-eight degrees. She knew what was wrong. He was afraid. Nervous. She could smell it from far way. The scent of fear and desperation fill with lungs as she let out a slow dragging exhale. And she loved it.–Hell, she wanted it. The feeling of satisfaction was so sweet to her that it left Onyx with a toothache sometimes. But this pain; this ache was different. It was mind-numbing, excruciating even, and she knew why the hunger was starting to get to her. *How long had it been?* When was the last time you had anything to eat other than human substance?

The taste of fear was the most intoxicating sense known to her kind. She had to admit, she was addicted. The fear coming from her teacher had taken over everything she knew. The drive from the scent alone made her focus on the lesson and more importantly –on Mr. Rocnard. Meeting his glance made him uneasy and the unsettling feeling of his eyes locking with her was enough to make her throat burn. The addiction was the only thing that she crave. It was everything and the only thing that she wanted. But she could not risk it—not now with so many witnesses. She needed to leave or she would expose herself to the entire room.

Without even getting permission, Onyx left the room and slowly made her way to the pale and plastic washroom. As she left the lecture hall, she felt numb. Nothing. Cold. Empty. The cold water hitting her face didn't seem to calm down her mind. She knew it would not quench her thirst. Onyx could never seem to control herself, even though it had been almost eight months since she had her fill of any human. She knew that it would not get better; that she would not get better until she quenched the agonizing pain. The pain would go away for a moment, but guilt and depression would soon follow. But she had always felt that way, ever since that night. And he was to blame.

Cairo, Egypt– 1952
Fire is the Eyes

It ended almost as soon as it began; the once beautiful paradise was now turning into an abrupt dystopia. The palm trees against the Nile were slowly dying when the flames came into contact with them. Pillars were crumbling against the sandy winds.

As the fires began to ignite the roofs, first she tried to get away from the other citizens. Three victims already laid limp against the ground soaking the sand with blood. He didn't care who he hurt as long as he got his prize—her. The dancing flickers rose into flares of destruction as the wind picked up. He would destroy villages, cities, and even the most beautiful places just to capture her. And this village was no different from the others that he ruined. What was once the beautiful utopia of Cairo, Egypt was becoming a puff of smoke and ashes. It had been almost a decade since she ran away from her fate, from him, but once again, he'd found her. It was almost second nature for her to flee from his clutches and for him to hunt her down—just like he always did.

Alexander stood on top of the broken white pillar as if he were a vengeful god. After everything he had done to draw her out into the opening, one might believe that he was god searching for his beloved, but he was searching for retribution not affection. As Alexander grabbed Mea, he slammed her into the pure bricks, leaving a bloody imprint into the wall and a gash on her forehead. Mea would not have kept her balance if it had not been for him pulling her arm.

"I promise I won't hurt you, unless you ask me to." He wanted to hurt her as a solution for running away time and time again. As he pulled away from the barely conscious body, he whispered to her, "I really wish you would accept what I have to offer. Maybe I would not have to pursue you on this never- ending game of survival. If only you would just stay with me. If only you could learn your place, my pet."

Mea tried to crawl away from the scene only to have Alexander kick her head into the broken statue of the sun god. "But like any animal trying to defy the master, you must be taught a lesson. A lesson that I will make sure sticks this time."

"If only…if only you would just stay by my side," Alexander said as he grabbed a handful of her long raven-colored hair. He sighed as he lifted her up by the throat. "But it seems that no matter how many times I ask you not to run from me, to accept what you are and become what I have taught you—"

Before he could finish, Mea spat a wad of blood in his face; it satisfied her, but only made her punishment worse. Alexander grabbed her left arm and began to yank it out of the socket. Mea screamed and tried to pull her arm away from the fiend's grasp, but it was hopeless; the more she struggled the more he pulled until the sound of her arm ripping from her shoulder echoed in the burning deserted valley. The bloodcurdling scream shattered what was left of the dying village.

"No one will ever accept you for what you are. I am all you have in this world, and yet you continue to surround yourself with these vermin. See how the others ran away after they saw what you did to the pharaoh's scribe. None of them even blinked an eye when I tossed you into the Nile River. It's truly sad how cowardly humanity has become, don't you agree, my pet? Fight or flight indeed. But that is their nature—to fear everything around them. Just like ours is to fight them at every turn. Survival justifies every mean and every opportunity."

Mea realized that no matter what Alexander was, every word he uttered was the truth; he would always be right. They didn't even flinch when she cried out in help. She was a novice to the minds of human beings, even when she was one she'd never truly understood them. The moment Mea begged for forgiveness—for mercy—all of them turned their back to her. The pitiful creatures would rather save their own hides then help someone in need. The need to survive did not matter to them.

They saw her as a killer—as a freak, not of nature but of something else. Against everything they believed in. Not one of them batted an eye to help.

"Let him torch this forsaken place to the ground. Everyone I ever cared about is gone anyhow. Nothing matters anymore. I can start over. It would not be the first time I had to start over. Pick up the pieces that shattered in my hands. It would be all over soon."

"I hate them. Go ahead and destroy this place. I don't care. You'd be doing me a favor, Alexander. I hate all of them. Why do they always look to me as if I'm the cause of everything wrong or every little misfortune that comes," she cried and screamed into his shoulders.

"It's because you are little kitten," he said as he bit into her shoulder. "Everything that is laid out in front of you crumbles under your fingertips."

But it was all in her mind. She never left the room. The thought of standing up towards her so called teacher made her thirst for his fear. As twisted and tempting as she was by the vision, she refused the thirst that began to burn inside her throat. As she forced herself to stay seated in her desk she began to grip the edge of her chair until her knuckles turned red. Never once moving an inch towards the door or the professor-that was now blowing and heaving his breathes as if he was going to have a seizure.

Every breath he took-every gasp he made brought Onyx closer towards the edge of her seat as well as her sanity. Just as the school bell rang and she was about to get out of her seat, Onyx heard a faint whistle come from behind her. At first, it started as a whisper in the winds that only she could make out. It was familiar but fleeting. The whisper grew into a whistle that would not stop until she halted in her tracks. It soon turned into a melody that sparked a memory. Not just a memory but all of her memories that rang from every country, every part of time she'd run to. That sound made every nerve in her body tense up. Shivers slid down her spine as the tone became more and more familiar to Onyx. No one could have known that tune, but no one in the room or the halls seemed to hear it. The faint ringing in her ears caused one of them to slowly start bleeding. Onyx pulled her handkerchief out of her pocket to quickly wipe the substance away. The last thing she needed was someone to notice and ask questions, for someone to try and care. The bell disrupted the melody and gave her an opening to leave the room before anyone else.

And as she ran into an empty classroom, the whistling grew louder and more unforgiving. It was torture just hearing it. The low bass of the sound began to climb higher to a frequency that could kill any animal that was near. But then suddenly it grew quiet.

Not here, not now. I covered my scent. Not here of all places. I concealed every trace of myself since I've been in this town. As she closed her eyes and focused her energy, she could feel the presence of another, someone not human. Someone who was actually similar to her. Room 1113 was to the far end of the hallway and usually locked because there was no one—teacher or student—who wanted to use the room. Onyx turned the doorknob and found that it was not only unlocked but there had been left open a crack.

"Dirty little game we play. Must it always come to this?"

Onyx whispered as she stepped into the room. She was trying to bait her enemy closer. *'Lurking in the shadows, trying to toy with others feelings and abilities; it's a little beneath you, isn't it? Traidor. We both know your little shadow games do not frighten me. I figured after so many years—decades—we would have gotten past this dance. You should be ashamed of yourself, Caleb. Hiding from me…it almost hurts my feelings.* Almost, she bitterly choked.

Chapter Two

Tango of Sins

'Like I care at all about your feelings.' The thought pressed against her senses.

Suddenly a young man stepped out of the shadows. "Well, well; if it isn't my little kitten come to spend some quality time with me. Do you know how hard it was to sniff you out…took me months to track you down? It warms my heart to see you here," he said with a smirk on his face and sarcasm in his heart. Shadows began to dance across the room, one of Caleb's parlor tricks that Onyx never found entertaining.

"I never would have guessed this is where I would find you. Who would have believed that you'd return to Massachusetts—let alone Boston? It brings back memories, doesn't it?" That smile always gave Onyx chills. Dressed in all black, except his white tennis shoes and the matching motorcycle jacket, Caleb was the last person Onyx wanted to see. He had caused so many problems throughout the centuries, and each seemed worse than the last. Fires that cascaded in the country sides. Murders turning up in every alley and dark part of her mind. She wanted him to leave her alone, but every time he appeared, she felt her heart stop.

Spanish Influenza (Germany)
1918

"GET THAT MAN TO THE infirmary, now." Elizabeth had tried not to faint at the sight of the newest and youngest patient that had been admitted into the hospital. The little boy, who went by the name of Ezre, was burning hotter than any normal patient that had entered the building. Every nurse was making bets to see how long the boy would live.

It may seemed horrible, but it was the only way the other men and women felt normal. . It disgusted her to no end how some of these people could call themselves nurses or doctors' aids.

"Come on, Liz, what do you think? Will he last the night," one of the unfamiliar male nurses said as he made his way past the others. Elizabeth had always thought the game of Live or Die was as childish as pulling wings off a pitiful insect that could not defend itself. None of them knew how precious and short life was, and probably never would. The hospital was a shelter for the thought of the final moments of life. A beacon of hope to the last strand of humanity that ours clung to in their time of reckoning. But Elizabeth knew better she had seen every face that the monster had brought and acknowledged every presence and victim that was taken before her very eyes.

"Get out of my face, Demetri. I don't have time to play you and everybody else's stupid, idiotic games. I have patients to take care of and save, maybe instead of playing God as if you can do his work and do your bloody job", Elizabeth said as she pushed past the others. The young tot, Ezre, had bunked with an elderly man that was wheezing against his pillow. She started with the older man, giving him a sedatative to keep him calm and help him get some rest. Just by looking at the elder she could tell he did not have look until he saw the graces of his haven.

She knew the young boy would be miserable the moment they placed him in the room. He could not stop crying and could barely breathe. She laid his head into her lap and stroked his short blondish hair. His skin became sicklier and paler as the minutes ticked by.

'I can save him,' Elizabeth thought as she looked down into Ezre's eyes. Green. 'The most beautiful green I have ever grazed upon.'

"Miss, you are going to save me, right? I have to go to see my mom after you treat me. She will be worried if I don't get home. Miss, I trust you." Elizabeth could not look the little boy in his eyes and lie to him, but she almost could not tell him the truth. That he may not make it through the night. The truth that he would never get to see his family again. He would never get to see his mother again. So, she did what anyone would do. She gave him hope.

"I will do my best, sweetheart, to make sure you see your mother. I promise, but you have to be a good little patient for me, okay?" He nodded with all of his might as he began to cough up blood.

"Little Ezre, I am going to give you something to help you sleep." She took out her handkerchief and began to wipe the blood away. As Liz turned away from her wry patient she felt a chill in the air; the presence of death was brushing against her spine. But she knew better he had come.

"How long have you been there," she said as she exhaled the bitterness from her voice. It was hard to be kind to her patients with him around. Let alone give the little boy a sedatative to keep him asleep for the night. He made her uneasy around medicines. Weeks ago she had given a woman the wrong dose that almost sent her into shock. Before long whenever he began to appear she drew further away from more of her sicklier patients, dreading not to make any mistakes. But this time she had made a dire mistake that could cost Ezre his life or worse.

He had stolen a nurse's robe and uniform to walk around without being noticed. The females probably gawked at him for a moment before returning to work, but not long enough to notice that he didn't belong there.

"Oh, come on—what are you going by now? Liza…Bethany…"

"My name is Elizabeth, you pompous traidor. And I would appreciate it if you did not cause a scene in front of anyone at this time," she sniped as she snatched a needle form his grasp. He could not help but laugh, she cared more about her reputation as a nurse than his actual presence before her.

"It's really cute to see you play doctor—"

"I'm a nurse and a doctor's aide—you moron." Elizabeth whispered as she began adjusting Erze's bedding. He was starting to sweat more and more, so that by the time that night fell the night nurse would have to change his bedding as well as his clothing. "What do you want here? I do not have time for your games. I have people to take care of."

"Like I said, it's cute to see you play doctor…sorry…nurse. I thought I would see your handy work and how thirsty you have become around all these miserable and frightened patients of yours."

"I've already eaten, Aubrey, but thank you for your concern." Elizabeth moved to the elderly man and began to take his tempature for the last time for the day. She knew that the doctor could not save him because of his age and all the other factors that made his symptoms worse; had he come in sooner or been a little bit healthier there may have been a better chance to save his life. After the sedatative that she had given him kicked in, it would be no problem for his next nurse to make the final arrangements for him. She could never do it. Not to anyone of her patients. Elizabeth would rather play ignorant to what happened next and think that they either overcame the flu or died in their sleep. Peacefully.

"So the old man is gonna die. Good thing I didn't bet with those other nurses, huh? They thought and hoped you could save the poor bloke." Aubrey paused. "But you and I know better. The only one you could have save—you just lied to in order to make him more comfortable,"

Aubrey said as he grabbed a handful of her black hair and kissed it. "So noble of you, in this dark time, in their dying hour of need. You truly are a healing spirit."

But as she looked at the four walls that surrounded them, she did not feel noble. She harbored a feeling of uselessness; of all the times that he could kick her when she was down he chose this time…

"Why are you doing this? At any time, you would have beaten me to a bloody pulp but you choose this time to be a concerned citizen. Why?"

Aubrey looked from the elderly man to the young boy. "How long does the old buzzard have to live?" Elizabeth strained her eyes at him in anger.

"His name is Richard. He doesn't have long though. One of the nurses will be coming in after my shift and will give him something to help him die in his sleep. They are calling it a *mercy killing*." Aubrey passed near the boy's cot and ran his hand over his head.

"You know you could save the kid. Not as a nurse, but as the kind of creature that is not a human being. The old man is doomed, his age alone would destroy his metal stability and anyone else's that tried, but the boy he's young a little gamey and scrawny. If you try and if you are strong enough you could save him." Elizabeth fell in the chair in between both of the cots.

"What are you talking about? Tell me how can I save Ezre? Please. Aubrey, you have to help me save him."

Aubrey began to laugh. "Oh, Lizzie, it's really simple. Drain him… drain the boy dry up until you have stopped his life force. And once you have his heartbeat so close to that brink, give him a piece of your essence." Elizabeth could hardly believe what he was saying. The procedure would not help either of them, not her, nor Ezre—at some point, anything could go wrong. It could either kill her or kill the boy.

"So what's your choice, Elizabeth? Save the boy and have someone at your side as a son, or leave him to die. It is your choice."

In the end, she knew she could not save the little boy. Onyx did not have the type of power to save him from the virus and could have contracted the flu herself. Ezre had survived the influenza for about a week before the virus broke down his nervous system as well as his motor skills that he could barely function. Demetri had refused to put the little boy to sleep because of his age. The one time the bastard finally gave any type of empathy and he choked up. Elizabeth and one of the doctors had found him bellowing in the garden, begging them not to make him do it. Not to a child.

Elizabeth almost cold clocked him for his hypocrisy. In the end, Elizabeth had to be the nurse to do it. She could not sleep for the rest of the month. To this day, Onyx still had nightmares about the little boy taking his last breath in her arms. In the end, Caleb only wanted her by his side to make her see that it was necessary to destroy as well as save humans' lives. She knew that it was all just a ploy to trick her.

He wanted her by his side, but every time she refused, he beat her senselessly until he became bored. He only time he refused was with Ezre. For that moment she almost believed that he wanted her to save the young lad. That was until he mocked and beat her sensibly for being spineless and letting the boy die-without even taking some of his essence before his departure.

"I don't have time for you, Caleb, so whatever it is that you want, I cannot and WILL not help you with your sick and sadistic games. I have had enough of you for more lifetimes than I have lived."

There was no courage in her voice as she stalked away only fear and remembrance. And as she walked off, he quickly stepped in front of her. As he slowly placed his hand on her shoulder, Onyx tried to move away, but he grabbed ahold of her with a firm, tight grip.

"See, that's the thing; and in one swift movement, he slammed her against the wall. "I don't care about what you think I want, because you will do as you are told. We both know that you are not as strong as you think and you can't fight me. But I will give you this that was some powerful stuff there, had me going. But we both know better don't we… it's all a façade. You have never been strong enough to put up much of a fight against me. Hell, you have not had your fill since Cairo, have you, little Mea? You forced yourself to feed and damn near kill others in Germany just so you could try and save those miserable creatures in the hospital. And every time you tried you failed. I am stronger than you and I will kill you if you keep disobeying me, so please, kitten, and stop pushing what little of my patience that I have left. There is no point in trying." He chuckled as he pushed pass her. "You have not even collected the essences and created the demented? You couldn't save Ezre, now could you? After you promised that poor soul that you would get him healthy again to see his dear mother. Did you ever tell him that she died weeks after they come to the hospital? Damn shame that her heart gave out like that. Did not even carry the will to steal his essence now did you? So how can you possibly even think to threaten me when you don't even have the strength to stand on your own two feet? So,"—Caleb paused as he brushed her hair away from her eyes—"why don't we get something in that stomach of yours? Why not that teacher of yours that perspired every time he looked at you. You would not believe the thoughts in that one's mind. "Ugh," Caleb shuttered distastefully. "Just plain filthy. The images that I saw were just plain-disturbing. And you think I'm sick." Caleb chuckled. He kissed her cheek and smoothed her hair back into place. But as Onyx tried to move away from his touch, she made one mistake: she slapped his hand away from her.

"No, I refuse to help you, or even follow you."

Caleb blocked her way out with the palms of his hands, threatening her.

"See you act so superior to me, but we both know you are just as twisted as the day I created you. So do what you were taught."

"And what am I supposed to do, huh," Onyx challenged. "Torment and mask their dreams like you do, or maybe stalk the women and men, manipulating and forcing them to believe that we are bloody saints, when you and I both know that we are nothing that any human could dream of without screaming in terror; we are far from the little lies that you tell you victims while they sleep. We are disgusting monsters that belong in the shadows. That demented power you use is just a sick and pathetic attempt to scare me, but I'm not going with you, Caleb." Suddenly, he backhanded her.

"Don't make yourself seem so holy. When I found you, there with nothing, not even a breath of air in your lungs. You are so ungrateful. Maybe I should have left you there on the streets to die," he hissed. "Everything and everyone had touched your skin, and you welcomed them. It's a shame our brother looked at you as if you were such a beauty. Always thinking you were pure. Hell, I'll admit it, there were times I, myself thought you were too. But you still believe that you are so much holier than me— don't you—that you don't need what I can offer you. That you don't need me…See that's your problem," Caleb said as he pushed her into the next room and closed the door behind them. Without warning or hesitation, he slammed her into the wall and sank his teeth into her flesh. Onyx knew she had gone too far. The buttons she had pushed made Caleb not only obsessed with making her feel undeniable pain, but to remember that no matter where she ran, any place that she tried to hide, he would destroy her. He grabbed her waist and lifted her to the desk. She knew never to try and squirm away, it would only hurt more, and he sank deeper into her flesh and nerves. She learned that lesson the hard way in Peru. It took three months before the tissues reformed back to normal. The room was spinning and Onyx felt absolutely nothing. Onyx began to zone in and out of consciousness as Caleb drained more and more of her blood and life. They both knew he did not need to bloodlust. When Caleb bloodlusted or even began to bloodlet it was to fill the hungry and quench the thirst that many individuals' souls were not strong enough to provide. With Onyx he never needed that formality. It was always to teach her a lesson in humility and for her to learn respect. Sure, the physical wound would go away, but the energy she was losing was mind-numbing and worse than death itself. As Caleb retracted his fangs, he kissed her gently on the neck and forehead, reminding her that she could feel whatever emotion he wanted her to feel. Sorrow. Pain. Pleasure. Happiness. He could leave her completely lost and shattered. And that was how he always left her—that was the enjoyment he found whenever he and Onyx were near one other. He loved making her his victim and causing as much pain and damage to her life as possible. Onyx would love nothing more than to be rid of Caleb; to be free.

She fell off the desk and began to scream. The pain had finally come. The senses always returned when Caleb disappeared. The sound of her screams rang throughout the halls, but no one would come. No one ever did. The smell of copper blended into the salt of her tears. The loss of blood impaired her vision; the only thing she could see was the blurry shifts of images as she tried to pull herself up. She lay there in her blood and tears, wishing for any sign of hope…

It was never ending, she thought as she left herself off the floor.

She stared out of the classroom and into the window and saw rain. In the pouring raining, she saw a figure staring back at her.

Not Caleb, she thought to herself. That psycho will not torment or stalk me like the others. He would rather I know he is around than have me paranoid and thinking someone is following me.

Whoever this figure was saw the whole thing and knew about them. Onyx could feel that person's energy, and it was stronger than Caleb's. With a smirk, she brushed off her white blouse and smeared away the blood to the point of evaporation. She grabbed her short black jacket and closed the door behind her, leaving the room as if nothing happened. The only people that knew about it were Caleb, herself, and the mysterious figure—who would become her new ally, whether either of them liked it or not.

Chapter Three

Blank Slate

THERE WAS NO POINT IN going home. Onyx didn't really have one. What she had was a condo right above the club she worked at, The Last Resort. The club was open twelve hours a day and open every day except the holidays. The owner or owners of The Last Resort were probably out for the day, but there was probably at least one worker both inside and outside the building. At times there would be more than two bartenders and a server but after issues with the last worker the owners decided that two bartenders was enough for the hole in the wall bar.

The outside of the club was a redeveloped abandoned building that looked as if it was condemned. It took almost two years to refurnish and finish both the inside and out, but most of the buildings in Massachusetts blended in with the beautiful scenery, and The Last Resort was no different. With its grounded red and white brick layout there was no way anyone could confuse the building with anything else. Especially since there was a scheme of graffiti on side wall. The painting is depicted of a black crow slowing dispersing into a flutter of feathers. The painting was so admired that it not only became the icon of the bar but many of its patrons don tattoos of the familiar scheme.

As she walked towards the structure it always fascinated Onyx the way some mortals were able to give perspective towards the talent of another-when they had none of their own. She had many talents before she became a runner, but those memoires and memories were so distant that they seemed like a fleeting impossible dream. And Onyx had better things to do than to dream impossible dreams. Survival was the main objective that kept her from passions even relations that she could have explored, but after a while it became boring and dangerous-when Caleb intercepted her path.

Loren was standing outside, pretending to be the bouncer, as Onyx walked up. Loren was Onyx's height, but there were several differences in there appearances: where Onyx had purplish black hair, Loren had dirty blonde with red streaks. Where Onyx's eyes were a jaded green, Loren's irises were clouded and stormy grey. Both young women were slender and could bench press as much as any man. Loren had black nail polish and Onyx had pale beige. Today, Loren decided to wear a black long-sleeve shirt, cut at her elbows, and a pair of blue jeans that were cut in the front and the back.

"New pair of jeans, chica," Onyx gestured as she opened the door. Loren followed suit and commented.

"They were, until some bitch decided that she wanted to fight me. I swear, there is no type of decency or respect in this time. The seventies had more respect than this time, even though it was filled with mobsters and lowlifes. This time…" Loren gagged as she looked down at her jeans in disgust. "There is just no decency, and the clothes are either too short or too tight. I hate when chicks fight dirt, grabbing my pants leg! Hell, she even tried to grab my hair. Is it so hard to fight fair or even clean for that matter? There is no civility at all. Really, what are you four," Loren said as she tossed a bottle of bourbon on the counter.

"And what did you do, oh child of peace," Onyx snickering sarcastically.

"I kicked her ass and took fifty bucks out of her wallet." Onyx shook her head in shame and grabbed two glasses. "Hey, she owed me a new pair of jeans. What was I supposed to do?"

As Loren was pouring their glasses, Onyx's got hers snatched from her. "Aren't you a minor," the bouncer, Elliot, joked as he tossed it back. He stood at least several inches past six feet with buzz cut black hair he was more than enough to handle the drunks that come and go from Last Resort.

But he was a consisted pain for Onyx to deal with. The bickering and mocking were the latest of his pranks that Loren called a "tasteful crush". Onyx saw it as bothersome and irritating badgering. That was one of the many cracks and jokes she received for pretending to be a teenager in high school. But it could not be helped she would never look any older than that of a seventeen year old- she was lucky enough that the owners believed Loren and hired her as a server as well as a bartender. Not that it mattered they were hardly in their own establishment. Onyx pushed the bouncer aside, but not before giving him a gesture with her pinkie finger.

"What's that for?"

"It's the feather, because you don't deserve the whole bird."

"You are so juvenile. Don't you have anything better to do then make trouble? Hell you should still be in school; that is if you hope to graduate."

"No, I just want your pretty face to look at ev-er-y-day." Elliot slowly walked away from the two women with a chuckle.

"You know what, I'm going outside. I don't have to put up with this; they don't pay me enough to deal with the two of you before opening."

"Okay, you two, back into your corners and come back for round two." Loren loved getting in between the spats, it made work entertaining. As she pushed Onyx back behind the bar and began to clean the shot glasses. Everything was quiet until Elliot came back and brushed Onyx's hair back. Normally it was his way of making peace with her but something struck a nerve with him, and she could not understand why until he placed his finger above her collar bone. Wincing in pain she realized that Caleb's love bite still hadn't faded yet. This time he'd wanted to leave a mark. He wanted someone to notice the mark. It was always painful and embarrassing when he left his bite mark, and even harder to hide then the bruises. Last week, she had to convince the school nurse not call her house about the bruise she'd found on her abdomen. Loren may be her guardian on paper, but she'd become the mother of the pack in a heartbeat the moment she found any knowledge or proof of Caleb doing any damage to her. She still had not told Loren that he was in town.

"Well, what is this? Seems our little virgin has finally found a suitor. So who is that unlucky solider that wounded you," Elliot said with a chuckle.

"Oh, you know what, shut the hell up… Wait, what's your name again?" Onyx questioned, and Loren burst into laughter.

"You know what, maybe I should find your new toy and warn him not to stay with you. Evidently, you don't know how to treat a man."

"That's not really a good idea," Onyx muttered as she kept her gaze away from Elliot. Ever since she moved here, he had always protected both her and Loren. The wisecracking and put-downs were just his way of being an overbearing big brother, and Onyx didn't mind it. She was afraid of what would happen if and when she had to leave this town. Loren would follow her and make sure that she was okay, but what about Elliot? Would he show the same gesture or would he becoming the alpha male she and Loren knew he could be and hunt down Caleb? She didn't want to lose another friend. Not toe that monster.

Onyx had finally found some peace of mind in this town, but it seemed as if she would have to pack up and leave again. She just needed more time. She didn't want to be on the run again, but she knew that it was inevitable. Her kind were nomads, but she'd always needed to make roots for herself. It was the only way she knew to feel a little human. She did not know what she would tell Loren, what reason she would have to give to ensure she would be okay. But she knew Elliot was a whole different case. He would not accept the good byes and farewells for no reason. He would want an explanation, and if it sounded like crap, he would make her stay. Running was always easy for her—the problem was making herself leave and cut ties with everyone she cared about before Caleb came to destroy everything. So it was best to keep it quiet for a while.

If he found out that Caleb had been at the school beating her senselessly, he would track the traitor down himself. Elliot had a code against any man laying a hand on any woman, and was not afraid to express that code. "Don't worry about who gives me what, okay; it's not like you own me."

Before Loren or Elliot could comment, someone walked into the bar. He stood at six foot even with a lean and tone frame. His blond hair was covering his eyes as well as his ears. He wore a red shirt that called for attention—brand new and fresh out of the store, black jeans, and black tennis shoes. As he walked over to the bar, Onyx started to feel his essence; it was sweet, which meant he had experienced life to the fullest, but it was sour, which expressed that he was not happy with his present condition—whatever it was. It was a rare combination: bittersweet. It hit her like a freight train.

Loren glanced at Onyx and they nodded in agreement. They both needed a fix, but which should take the first bite. Onyx was only okay with feeding as long as Loren was there to make sure she didn't go too far. Many of their kind had a knack for seeking out more than one essence, which led to overfeeding or even poisoning the victim, but it was normal. Onyx's condition was not what many would find or even call normal—one essence every blue moon; it was a surprise she was still breathing. Sheltering the beast and the hunger was never easy and having a rare filet steak dangled in your sights did not make the thirst burn any less. He slid a twenty-dollar bill on the table and glanced from girl to girl, looking them in the eyes. He could not see the layer of hunger that both ladies hide with ease. On the outside he saw two beautiful women that could and would help him get a drink-but on the inside there were two ravenous fiends ready to devour his very soul.

"So which one of you are gonna serve me? I don't have all day."

"A little stuck on manners, are we? But I'll let it slide 'cause you're cute. What can I get you?" Loren winked as she flipped a shot glass and a regular glass on the counter. "What's your poison, sweetheart?"

Show off, Onyx said, laughing, in Loren's mind.

Like you wouldn't! He's the sweetest thing I've ever felt or smelled in a long time. I'm practically shivering to get a taste, and by the looks of it so are you. Besides, I have never had a risk-taker, and here is one right in our laps. Ugh I can smell his essence…. They say you can never tell what their aftertaste will be, and it changes after each feeding. My skin is just prickling against every hair just for a taste.

"So what are you drinking," Onyx said as she put the bill in the register. *Okay, I'll admit it has been a while since I've tasted someone that smelled like wine and dark chocolate. Hell, it's been a while since I've had a taste of anyone. My throat is burning just inhaling his scent. But I doubt I should try to have a taste right now; it's not near or even close to my feeding period.*

"I need to talk to the owner of this place." Loren and Onyx were both taken aback by the change of his tone. He was not buying a drink; he was buying information. And no one at this bar was a sellout.

"I'm sorry, but neither of the owners are here, but if you want, one of us can help you." Loren slid into Onyx's mind saying, 'What do you think he wants?'

Same thing as the rest, to buy Jena and Alex out, and he'll get the same response as the rest. Onyx glimmered as she smiled at their next potential meal.

We are not selling, get off my—our—property, they screamed into each other's minds. Jena and Alex were fraternal twins with the same destruction nature that glistened in their dead blue eyes. Jena wore her long blonde hair in a long braid that danced down her back. While her older twin Alex cut his hair not only to look professional but not to be confused as a younger version of himself. What they lacked in personal skills and humility they made up for in business and professionalism. They refused to sell any revenue in Boston. It was their home town and the bar belong to the late grandfather and was passed down to every child-if they wanted the rights. And no matter how much was thrown at them they never sold The Last Resort.

"I wanted to ask them about an employee of theirs, um…Olivia Traer." Onyx almost dropped the glass upon the floor. How did he know her?

Loren slid back against the bar countertop. "And why, pray tell, do you need to know?"

"Are you her?" He looked between both of them.

"Answer my question first, if you're a gentleman." Now Loren was getting upset—either he was stalling for another person to come into the bar or he was testing the waters. Either way, he was not going to make it out of the building alive. It would not take long before Elliot would sense the tense around the bar.

Onyx decided to defuse the situation. The last thing they needed was a dead tourist.

"That's me. I'm Olivia, why do you need to speak with me? Did I do something wrong?"

Onyx, what going on? Do you know this prick? Loren sneered cautiously.

I've never seen this guy until today. Maybe he's like us. It is not unusual to have a nomad pass by every so often.

But Loren had her reservations. *Then why didn't he use your real name? If he wanted to see you, he could have just come in and talked to us like normal. Instead, he is flashing money—money, by the way, he's not getting back. I don't like this at all. Something is very wrong with this guy. Risk-taker or not, he doesn't belong here, Mea. He needs to leave…now.*

Onyx knew that when Loren used one of her true names she meant business. *Hey, Elliot, we need a little muscle, if you could be so kind.* Elliot joined the conversation and began to worry.

What's the matter? I can feel you two panicking. I figured you both would be feeding off the poor sod.

Loren sent the message to the bouncer's mind and he stepped into the building. *He is asking too many questions for my liking and I want him out.*

"Is there a problem?" Elliot said as he leaned his body against the wall. *You two okay?*

"And may I ask who you might be?" the guy asked.

"Elliot—name. Bouncer—occupation. Hobby—kicking and beating the living crap out of those who harass ladies hard at work. What's your business here? And why are you bothering my bartenders?"

"That's really none of your concern, Elliot the bouncer," the stranger retorted as he turned back to the bartenders. But Elliot was in no mood. He grabbed the chair and pulled the smart aleck up to within inches of his face.

"You've got two options, worm: a. either buy yourself a drink and sit so quietly that I can't even hear you breathe, or b. get the hell out. If you piss any one of these girls off I'll make sure you wouldn't be able to pick yourself off the floor."

"I'm pretty sure all three of you would want to hear what I have to say." Elliot lifted the man by the shirt and tossed him on his back onto the bar's countertop. "I'll say again, what's your fucking business here?"

"Okay, my name is Damien, and I'm looking for Olivia. I need to talk to her, it's very important. And I'm pretty sure she'll talk to me. She's is the only one who can help me; at least that's what he said."

Onyx came from the back of the bar with Loren following. "Who told you about me? Who told you to seek me out?"

"Can you get your muscle to let go of me? I can't talk with two hundred pounds of rage on my ass." Damien let out a breath as he tried to move.

"Elliot, it's okay, you can let him go." And with that, he did but not gently. "Now, who told you my name, and why are you looking for me," Onyx said as she grabbed the front of his shirt and pushed him against the edge of the bar.

"He told me, that his name, but I doubt that's what it is."

"Spit…it…out then," she said, gripping her teeth against her lips as she began to draw blood.

Damien tried to wiggle out of her grasp but realized it was only going to get tighter.

"Wow, you're strong for a chick, you know that?" He was trying to make a joke out of the situation. But Onyx was in no mood for laughter.

Elliot began to rolls his eyes at the wise crack, "You know normally I would remark saying something like "You can't spelled slaughter without laughter", but buddy if you thought that I was trouble; you got it wrong. Don't piss off the ladies making your drink."

"Either you tell me a name or I'm gonna get a whole lot nicer," Onyx said sarcastically as she glared, pushing her other hand to the base of his throat.

"He said his name…his name is Benjamin…that's what he called himself."

Do you know anyone by that name? Elliot's words ran through her mind like a freight train. He was afraid for her and didn't want to lose one of his only friends. He had already lost so much when he came into their world. Most of the nomads lost their families and friends long before the change, but Elliot was one of the unlucky ones to lose everything before, during, and after his change. His protective nature toward both of the girls was both comforting and yet frightening if anyone threatened them.

Yeah, chica, do you even know a Benjamin? Loren scanned her friend's memories. Onyx never minded when she did it—sometimes it was easier for her, then, to explain what was going on in her life. She and Onyx had known each other for nearly two hundred years and the name held little value to her. But Onyx didn't have to trace back her history, or her lives. His face would never leave her.

I know who it is. Onyx flashed them both her memories.

The fires that broke out in Cairo before the Great War. The influenza of Spain and the New World. The settlement of the French Quarters. The late night walks during the Ripper murders. He always changed his name but never his features. Benjamin was his favorite because it disguised his true nature, and what he really was a killer. He seemed like an intellectual scholar that would and could always be trustworthy, the image of a nobleman and a saint, but his true nature screamed savage. He was a cold-blooded murderer. Brutal and unmerciful toward any and all that tested him and his rage.

"Damien, tell me what Benjamin really told you. Because I really, truly doubt that he didn't give you more than just his name. Benjamin is not a man of few words, and I'm pretty sure you didn't come here all the way to Massachusetts on a word of mouth alone."

Damien studied each one of them before pulling out three pictures. The first was an old pinup picture of a young woman during the late 1920s. Black and white though the picture was, the image was breathtaking. The woman looked mid-teens, almost early twenties, with a smile that seemed to light every corner in the picture. Her hair pinned up, wearing a beaded dress—gorgeous was the only description that fit her. Elliot gave a long whistle.

He pulled out a folded napkin that held a drawing of a girl with the similar smile, but with long, flowing black hair, wearing a long, flowing light blue dress. This sketching looked preserved.

The last was a more recent picture of the girl in a short white dress and her hair forced into a plait.

Damien brought his eyes back to see that each one of them was stunned. In amazement, confusion, and fear. "Now tell me what do all these pictures have in common?" There was silence. "All right each one of these three pictures is of the same woman. In a different time period." He stared down as he pointed. "1926, New York City." He placed his index on the first picture. "1767, Spain." The sketching. "And recently, two months ago in this little town of Boston. So—I'll tell you what I was told, but you won't like what I have to say. I can save you. "And there it was again, a life preserver drifting closer and closer to Onyx's sinking stomach. No one would think this true if it came from Caleb's mouth delivered by a risk-taking food source.

East End London – Whitechapel
November 1888

The night started to grow into the early morning as the fog began to spread. As the air shifted, Teresa draped her silk shawl tighter around her frame. Her clothing was particularly odd to be found in East End of London, but she had business to attend to. Teresa Maddison Livings wore a white and maroon colored dress with a bodice underneath. Some believed that it constricted most of the high society women, but Teresa was used to it. And it wasn't like she needed to breathe every second of every day. Her family had trained her to practice deep breathing, not only for church choir but also for the different corsets her mother bought from the foreign traders.

She left the matching petticoat at home for fear of overheating. Her outergown was a gorgeous maroon with threaded embroidery and the apron was lined with maroon lace. Unfortunately, Teresa had cut the bows off late last night, all except for the bow in the back that sat perfectly on her backside.

London's weather seemed to change with every turn of the corner, which was the main reason she left the coat at home. She wished that she had left the hoop skirt at homelike she had abandoned her gloves and bonnet. The streets were unbearably quiet, which was to be expected with the murders taking place. The Ripper, he called himself.

Such rubbish, Teresa thought to herself as she walked passed a streetwalker flirting with an older gentleman missing one of his front teeth. She had no feelings for the unfortunate. They didn't bother her nor did she pity them. They were in blissful ignorance of the world beyond wealthy and poverty. How she wished she could have that feeling again.

As she looked at the clock, she noticed that he was late. No doubt having his fixings before the police found the remains.

"You know, if you would come on time I would not have to wait. It's very ungentlemanly like and disrespectful."

Just then, a cloud of smoke and fog cloaked her feet and the fog began to whirl around the shadow in front of her.

"My apologies, young maiden, but this is not your scene nor is it your dwelling, is it? Isn't it past the lady's bedtime? What would your wardens think if they knew you were out in the shady underbelly at such an hour?" He chuckled as he wiped the blood from his cheek. No doubt, there would be another article in the paper about his shortcomings and mistakes. "Careless as ever and just as reckless like a pup that grew up without the proper training. Did you at least dispose of the body like you were taught? I would hate to see your master's face when he comes back from France." He began to snarl and show his canines. She apparently had stuck a nerve. They both know that his master, his creator, had deserted him after he'd embarrassed the both of them at a gala. After he had beaten the oblivious brute he took his leave to conduct business among trades.

"I do not have a master. My master is dead to me. The only thing I have left is the God in the afterlife and the beauties of Mary Magdalene that come at my very beck and call. I have not the likes or the desire for your company or any talk of the man that abandoned me."

Jack the Ripper, he called himself, or at least that is what the papers deemed him after the letters they'd falsified. He had no means of penmanship. The knowledge he had for surgery and medical skill was all he had left after his creator botched the procedure of the Ripper's new life. And even with that skill the gift itself was turned to malice and murder towards unsuspecting women of the night. His master made sure Cain gave the illusion of being a man of high quality.

"Cain," Teresa said, trying to reason with him. But he began to scream and shout. "My name is Jack. You know me only as Jack THE Ripper.

Do you understand me, you high-class harlot?" He pushed passed her in fury. "If only I could have you, but I was told not to. And every time I have an impure thought about you, it is like I have burning nails buried deep into my flesh. He is not my Master but his command is still in my head and it hurts to think of you. And for that I loathe you."

Despite the pain, Cain, or Jack, as he demanded to be called, began to step closer to Teresa. The burning look in his eyes signaled one clear objective: he wanted to make her his next victim. Suddenly, he was slammed against the brick wall opposite her. The movement was too quick and fluid for Cain to notice, but it was slow enough for Teresa to get a look at her savior. The thought of him being her rescuer made her give a snorted chuckle. The disgrace he created was not allowed near Teresa and he made a point to beat the command into his head and break his body if need be.

Dawning a red petticoat and a pressed white shirt made the dark-dyed pants a complete ensemble. He refused to wear a powdered wig because of the length and fullness of his light colored hair, which he tied in a low ponytail.

"I give you a specific order. One that I figured you would be smart enough to follow, despite what you lack. An indistinct command that not even you, a commoner with no intellect, could follow." He took a deep, hollow breath as he met his creation at eye level. "What do I find—not only are you defying me." He grabbed Cain by the throat, pulled him to his feet, and slammed him into the wall. "You are leaving a bloody mess at every corner of the East End. A muddled mess that she has to come and bring to my attention. Nothing but chaos that I have to tidy up like I'm your bloody handler. I tossed you to the dirt and cobble where I found you for a reason. Because you were a horrid disgrace to me, and I had no use for you at that moment if time."

The only thing that was sparing Cain's life was that Frederick was giving him a lesson and a scolding. Frederick wanted Cain to learn from his mistakes, but it seemed as though it fell on deaf ears.

"I am not going to listen to a puny man that takes orders from the society. If I want to break every Mary and Catherine that I see walking the streets with their legs strutting out, I will do so. And there's nothing the likes of—" In that instant, Frederick slammed his fist inside Cain's chest. Cain's body became limp as Frederick pushed him against the corner.

The police were not to worry about at this moment. Most likely, by now they had discovered Jack the Ripper's latest and final victim. The cobblestone ran red with the wine of Cain. Teresa had thought if she informed Frederick of his former project's behavior that he would try to convince him to stop to the devious and brutal murders, which had transpired in his absence. She never thought in her wildest imagination that he would put down one of his favorite pets. But Frederick was never predictable.

"Most unfortunate and I had high hopes for you. You skills in medicine alone rivaled every doctor and physician I have come across. The perfect tool and ally in this time where no man is welcome. Let this be a lesson; a pup that never obeys its master will be struck down until the hand is forced to end that pup's disobedience."

Chapter Four

Breath

On November 13, 1888, the murders of Jack the Ripper were brought to an abrupt end, and Cain's body was never found. Teresa never asked Frederick what he did with the corpse. She didn't care, as long as the murders came to the end. The only thing that plagued her thoughts and dreams were his motives and the type of women he chose.

As Loren began to lock the doors Elliot moved to the front of the bar and started to lock up as well. Onyx slowly began to put away all the alcohol and mixers, but she kept her eyes on the new guest. What Damien had to say did not need to be heard by others. The only thing that was left was to change the sign for the customers.

Last Resort was closed.

And all hope was abandoned.

Damien sat at one of the copper colored tables farther away from the bar. Elliot had suggested it after Loren threatened to break a bottle over his head.

"So he has an alias. I figured that out when I first spoke with him. I mean there's no way in hell he would have given his real name at the spur of the moment in the conversation. Especially when he kept shifting his eyes to the exits," Damien said as he lit his cigarette. Onyx always hated the taste of them. Even though they couldn't kill her, the thought of putting the white toxic paper to her lips made her gag. Yet the smoke was an attractive quality during the 40s: the daze, the illusion. God, how Onyx missed her life during the 40s.

"So what are you drinking, sweetheart," The bessie at the bar flirted. Not that it mattered; she wasn't Roxanna's type.

"I'll have a tonic with a side of your lips and your name of course," Roxanna smile as she passed her finger across the barkeep's mouth.

"Now, now sister. Don't play with your food. Especially when you are known to waste. The cherry blonde sat on the side of the raven-haired beauty and slid a box on the bar counter.

"Gypsy, I can't help it." Roxanna smiled. "She started it."

The charlie bartender smiled as she began to fill both the ladies' glasses with a blue and red liquid. "And my name is Natalie, by the way." She handed Roxanna a napkin with a red lipstick print on it. "But you can call me Tali."

Without attracting notice, a young man took a seat to Roxanna's left side. "Ahh, you really know how to pick them don't you, kitten? She is a feisty little soul isn't she? But what do you expect, so young, so full of life." She gazed into the cherie's eyes, laid a kiss on her fingertip. "Charm never escapes us. We use it for two things. When we want to, and when we have to…to get what we want."

Gypsy laughed as the cherie walked off. "I never thought I'd see the two of you fighting over a toy. Neither of you have the same taste in women." Roxanna glared, wanting nothing more than to stop this feud before the fire became more than anyone could handle.

"Tell me, James, when did you started picking up bartenders? I thought they were too easy for you."

He chuckled. "They're not easy, little kitten; they just work for tips."

"Yeah, he goes by different names. So what all did he tell you about me?" Onyx scowled as she pulled up her chair. He blew out a puff of smoke and swallowed the rest. The puff of smoke brought Onyx back from her memories. Disgusting.

Loren and Elliot had gone back to the condo; Loren could not be in the same room with such an appetizing essence, let alone with a "messenger" of Caleb's. She hated the bastard as much as Onyx did but their history went back much further. And Caleb would never let Loren forget. He brought her through the times as many insulting things. He used her as a slave during the Egyptian times, circa 800 BC. Loren was dubbed a mistress during the Golden Ages, and a concubine in Ancient Greece. Her pain didn't rival Onyx's but they both shared the pain and hurt of Caleb's madness.

"He met me when I was graduating and trying to work on my thesis of reincarnations. It was something that I had been working on since I was a sophomore, and he seemed very interested about my knowledge. I thought he was screwing with my head at first but after a while—and a couple of drinks—he seemed to care and take notice. He told me that if I wanted to find any answers, real proof, I should travel to Boston."

"Where'd you meet him?"

"On the campus in Ohio; he told me that there were many of the few that were born into different lives, but they could remember glimpses of their past. I had presumed that many saw their past lives during dreams, but I had never imagined what he spoke of was beyond my research.

That not only could there be someone that recalled their life, but could also branch out and pick someone from a crowd that was the same as them. He mentioned that you had nightmares and dreams like what my thesis was based on, and he said I should meet you. He gave me your information, where you went to school, where you lived and worked. I tried to go by your school, but they would not let me near your classroom because I was not a student nor was I a member of your family. I figured I'd just take a tour around Boston and see what the city had to offer and wait for you to come to work."

Onyx caught the twitch in his left eye. She smelled the truth, and what Damien was giving her was not it. Either he was telling her what he believed was the truth or he was lying and she could not find a lick of truth in his mind. Caleb might have coached him on what to say and what to do. He'd probably warned Damien about Loren's ability to read thoughts or memories. He had thought of everything, except that Onyx had learned how to smell senses, as well as traits like honesty. But Onyx was willing to probe the stooge for knowledge and information.

"So, what was this 'you could save me' bs?"

"He told me if I said something that one of your 'old' lives would remember, you'd talk to me. I believe that was what your first love during the 1940s told you…that was the name he gave me?"

"How 'bout dropping the details of my past. It's none of your concern nor is it Benjamin's." Onyx had to try not to choke on the name. His blood and soul began to pulse with the intensity that overpowered him. But no matter how much his adrenaline pumped, Onyx could still smell the fear and lies that he sweated out of his skin. She began to lick her lips in thirst. **So close.**

When was the last time I had a good soul to drain? November 2002? Or was it All Hallows' Eve? The night in Buenos Aires? Onyx pushed the memory of her first night with Caleb out of her mind; that was a memory of something that would never seem to end. She could never be that beast that Caleb desired, never again.

"Funny, what did he say about himself? That he already knew who I was, but we didn't get along. Benjamin and I aren't the closest of friends. He never writes or calls. Did he mention that to you? Or even how he met me?"

"To be honest, he didn't really speak much about himself. He sat in, the day of my presentation, and waited till everyone was gone, except the two of us. He asked me where did I get my research from and told me that I could get a true being to speak on whether this was all true or not. And he told me about you." Another lie.

"The thing is, Damien, I don't believe you. One, Caleb would not tell anyone about my past, even if his life depended on it." She quickly moved in and had Damien on the floor, and her elbow was in his chin, and her knee was in his rib cage, cracking the bones every time he moved. "So, you want to tell me the truth, or are you going to keeping lying? Because the more you lie, the harder I'm gonna push into your fragile bones, until you tell me the truth or until I hear every individual rib fracture and crack and snap while you internally bleed out every last drop of blood. So what's it gonna be?"

"Okay, okay, I'll tell you. Damn, please just don't hurt me." At that moment, a memory came to Onyx's mind and she could not push it away. The fear of that night had destroyed her. It would always haunt her just like Caleb would.

Chapter Five

Fire that Remains

IT WAS HARD TO COME back to the colonies, watching everyone go about their lives as if nothing was wrong. Women being hung for simple and ignorant crimes. Child becoming petty thieves and destroying what their mothers worked so hard to keep pure. Men walking away with everything they ever wanted, only to waste and lose it in one night. Massachusetts, the New World itself, started to become as dull and dysfunctional as the rest of the world. Amelia did not miss Lexington, and refused to go back to Boston, no matter how much they begged her. But tonight she had almost wished they had kept going; maybe the night would not have ended so horribly in disaster.

"Just do it, already." Benjamin paced back and forth and stomped with every turn he made. In his mind, swift and painless would have been the answer for everything, no matter what the reason. Mercy, to him, was a crutch that left nothing but feeble hopes and lost wishes. As his brother laid on the brink of death in an alley of Lexington, Massachusetts, all his thoughts left him. The only thing that mattered to him was leaving with Amelia, even if it meant leaving without his brother. "Amelia, we have to go. Now."

"What do you expect me to do, Benjamin? Let him die here and walk away?"

He stopped and looked to see if anyone was around. The town was silent, and at a quarter past one the only thing that broke the silence was the father clock that faced the middle of the town. The shutters of every house were either closed or the candle that was once burning in them was blown out. Silence was easy, so was hiding a body, but they could not leave him. Not their travelling companion and closest friend. At least she could not leave him.

"Of course not, Amelia, but we have to stop the bleeding. And we can't take the soul or the blood out without causing more pain." All of a sudden, the young man screamed out in pain. Blood seeped out of every hole on his face and body.

"Jarieck, please hold on," Amelia said as she pulled his head into her lap and began to sing to calm him down.

I don't know if you can see,

The changes that have come over me

In these last few days,

I've been afraid

that I might drift away…

Jarieck—even with his face full of blood—was beautiful. He had a light copper skin tone with brownish-yellow eyes that were shrouded by his black hair. His black petticoat and white slacks were soiled with blood and tears.

"Lady Amelia, Brother Benjamin, please leave me. We cannot risk the exposure to us all. They will find the body and go to our inn. Save yourselves and leave me behind. You must go." Jarieck coughed and hacked at every word. Even the gasp of air he took left him miserable. They knew he would not survive the night unless they did something. They only had two options:

"We are not leaving you to die. Please don't do this; do not ask this of us. Of me," Amelia cried as she tried to constrict and bind the soul. They could save him. The deceitful ingrate that tampered with the soul was experienced and knew exactly how to kill them, but Amelia knew how to counter it.

"What? Amelia, what are you doing?" Jarieck and Benjamin questioned deeply. "You'll kill us both, darling."

"I don't care," she screamed. "You can't leave us. You promised us, and you promised me. So please don't die. I'll do whatever it takes to keep you alive." Before she could finish, Benjamin tore her away from Jarieck.

"You impudent fool. Have you gone mad," Benjamin said, quarreling.

Amelia tore away from him and went back to his brother's side. "Let go of me, we have to save him. Don't you even care that your brother is dying!"

Benjamin pushed her into the street. "He made his choice. We warned him to stop making trouble and what does he do? Start a fight in a brothel and then find a royal son close to his engagement and decides to try and drain him dry. He had to be stopped, Amelia."

"What do you mean 'he had to be stopped'? What did you—"she stopped as she saw that Jarieck had died with no one at his side. She could not believe that they'd let their brother die.

"I'm so sorry, my love. For not telling you. Amelia, I love you and I want you to stay by Benjamin's side as if I never left. I will see you again." It was the last thought that he past to his loved ones. His brother that he trusted so much had brought along his demise. And all Amelia could do was weep in horror.

"You, you killed him, didn't you. How could you? He was your best friend."

"Yes, the best friend of mine that was not only betraying me by being with you but also feeding from you, Amelia. You were not supposed to lie with him. He was using your sympathy for him to convince you to let him feed," Benjamin said as he pushed her away from the body.

"So, where is the body he drained?"

"In the river—so drunk he accidently fell into the Hudson River. Tragic, really, and on the eve of his wedding. Such a shame to leave such a beautiful bride at the alter to mourn so young."

Amelia slammed Benjamin into the wall and tore at his flesh.

"Temper, temper, remember what you promised your lover." She let go of his flesh and spat the blood away. Vile, he was vile in her eyes now. Once friends, now bitter enemies, over a simple mistake.

"That was before you left him to die. Why? Why did you kill Jarieck, your only friend?"

"Because he loved you, and you were mine first." Benjamin flashed into her mind the night that they lay together and gave blood to one another. Before Jarieck had arrived in London and before she was even old enough to understand their bond. The laughter that they both shared flashed into her mind. The memories that he treasured slammed into her with every new thought. He hated that he loved her. That he trusted her. But he hated his brother more for stealing her from him.

"That was to keep you alive, you had not eaten in days, Benjamin. I was trying to save your life. You mean the world to me, but you did not have to kill Jarieck. We made a pact to look out for each other," Amelia sobbed. "And you dishonored the pact with your bloody masochistic hands!"

"And the kiss, the fact that within that moment I gave you what no other man could give you in your former life."

"Go to hell, I never want to see your face again and I wish I never knew that you existed. Good bye, Benjamin, I hope you enjoy your existence alone."

If I should become a stranger
You know that it would make me
More than sad
Caledonia's been everything
I've ever had

Chapter Six

Nomads

As Onyx came out of the memory, Damien was running away from her into the parking lot, trying to start his car. Onyx grabbed him by his throat before he could close the door, and pushed him away for the wheel.

"Get out of the car and drop the keys on the ground." He did as he was told and left the car. "Now tell me the truth." Just as Onyx was pushing Damien back into the club, Elliot and Loren were leaving the condo.

"What the hell happened to him?" Loren looked at Damien and laughed. "You scared him, didn't you?"

"No, he better be lucky I didn't kill him for being an idiot. He decided to run off and I was hit with an old memory."

Damien stared at her as if she spoke another language. "So you are a reincarnation. I don't believe it; he really did help my research." That comment earned him another slam into and through the bar's door by Elliot.

"What memory, Onyx?"

"London, 1769." That alone made her friends cringe in fear; that was the first of their kind to be killed by a companion. It was unspeakable. The first nomad had killed another out of self-defense a half a century later. It led many not to travel in packs and also not to trust others of their kind. It was the destruction of Caleb's sanity.

"He triggered it?"

"I don't think so. He was just there when it happened. But I doubt he did anything. But he does know something about Caleb that he won't bother to share."

Loren pushed past the two of them and stared into Damien's mind. The ability was easier to do with each other than humans, but Loren could slide into someone's mind as easily as water through cracks. The person would never feel it and never know she was there, but they would be left with a headache the next time they thought of the memory she searched for. The process usually took about thirty minutes, but once Loren was in, she felt the tug and released too quickly.

"I don't know who he is, but he isn't who he says he is."

"What do you mean? What happened?" Elliot said as he helped her up.

"I don't know, but the mind… I got close enough to something and he, or the memory itself, pushed me out. And the moment I tried to go back inside and find that memory I was thrown out like I was some kind of virus."

"Has that happened before?" Elliot supported her weight as he placed her on his back. He knelt down to the stool and let her sit down.

"Strangely enough, no, not even our own kind has had the ability to push me out…that is except for Caleb. Damn it all, Caleb must have given some of his blood to this idiot and now I can't breach him. This brat is more than just passing by, giving information. I think he might be a pupus from Caleb."

"What's a pupus and why are you shaking?" Elliot said with concern. Loren began to laugh as Damien slipped in and out of consciousness.

"I can't believe he is actually able to make a pupus. Jarieck really did not realize how strong his brother really was." Elliott grabbed a hold of her and forced her to look him in the eyes. The sheer terror that loomed between the two of them not only frightened Onyx, but it made her uneasy to believe that Damien was helping Caleb.

"What is a pupus, and why are you worried?"

Loren began to push away from Elliot. The fact that Caleb could do the unspeakable and go against everything amazed, scared, and disgusted her. He had been somewhat of a genius before the change and as the years turned to decades his power and abilities began to rival and surpass those around him. As her gaze fell upon the now-unconscious human, her thoughts lingered. She could kill him, send a message to Caleb to stay away from them, but what would that solve? Onyx placed her hand on Loren's shoulder and smiled. She wanted to protect her sister, but every minute that Caleb was still alive meant that it was only so long that Onyx would stay sane or alive herself. He needed to be stopped, no matter the outcome. "We should be worried. A pupus is what we use, puppets basically. They can come and go with no remorse, sometimes even no memory. Once a pupus has a thought or an order in its head, it will not stop until it sees everything through. They are the perfect weapon in both worlds. The humans would just either kill it or lock it up for its mental state. We would not be able to tell—most of us—and we'd think it's an ordinary human and feed, lowering our defenses to an attack, or worse. The scary thing is that Caleb can use all of the pupus' senses and thoughts and manipulate them to his advantage. And once the pupus is dead, the bond and connection between the two of them are severed." Onyx stared at Damien who was now awake, but she doubted he knew what they were talking about because he didn't even acknowledge them as he began to look around. Loren pushed Elliot aside and grabbed Damien by his shirt collar.

"Okay, start talking, 'cause unlike Onyx, I don't like listening to lies, and right now I am far from happy. And even more so, I don't like being tossed out of someone's head. So either tell us how you can block me out and how you know about Onyx, or so help me, I'm gonna—"

"Loren," Onyx said as she reached for the blonde's shoulder. "He doesn't know anything. Why else would Caleb shield him?"

Damien looked dazed and confused as he shuffled to the front door of the bar. The three would have thought he was a regular drunk, if they had not just met him hours ago, the way he was stumbling around the parking lot. He fell over and landed on top of the grass, vomiting out whatever had been in his stomach. Elliot walked over and picked him up as the girls opened the door to the club so they could take a look at him.

Chapter Seven

The Red Parade

ELLIOT TRIED TO PIECE TOGETHER everything that Loren had told him about Caleb and his newest project, Damien. He couldn't understand why Caleb would go to such lengths to destroy everything they all had worked so hard for. After Caleb had killed his best friend, Elliot swore that he would make him pay, but after years of being around normal humans, he was beginning to wonder what the point was. Death would come and life would begin; that was the philosophy of his life, his existence, and nature and natural order.

As he saw Onyx tending to the battered and bruised puppet, he could not help but feel a tinge of anger and bitterness. As kindhearted as she was, she was just too naïve, and that would one day get her killed.

"Hey, Elliot," Loren said as she pushed herself off the barstool. "Don't you think you've gawked at her long enough?" He grunted at her assumptions.

"Don't start, Loren. We don't need this, not now." Loren began to circle around him in wonder.

"I've always wondered why you have been so protective of us. Why do you even stay around? None of us are putting out anything for you and there's nothing for you to gain. But here you are the chivalrous knight in white armor. So…"

Elliot brushed passed her and turned. "It has nothing to do with that; it's just you both remind me of my little sisters. I lost them both. You and Onyx remind so much of them—whether you two are bickering or playing with bar glasses. I enjoy being around the two of you, nothing more." Elliot began to chuckle. "Hearing you call me a chivalrous knight reminds me of the medieval days." He looked back at Loren and began to sigh as he handed her a towel. Loren stared down at the black tiles and back up into Elliot's brown eyes. "What were their names?" But he never answered, he walked away and left Loren in her guilt.

Chapter Eight

Soul Shattering

IT HAD BEEN ALMOST THREE hours since they brought Damien to Loren and Onyx's condo. He had been passed out on the floor, puking out his guts. Elliot stared down at him. "Is that even normal?"

Loren shoved the unconscious traitor with her foot as he began to vomit again. After he tried to run away from her for the third time, Loren got tired of it and ran after him. It was simple, but the brute force of slamming Damien to the ground left him bruised and unconscious again, but not before he emptied out the remaining contents of his stomach.

"Yeah, it is normal for someone who tries to escape my search, but I think beside the fact that we cracked his ribcage and he might have a little internal bleeding, he should be fine." Onyx looked down at Damien and began to sing:

I don't know if you can see,

The changes that have come over me

In these last few days,

I've been afraid

that I might drift away....

Onyx almost felt a twinge of sympathy for Damien. He knew exactly what she had once gone through— being used by Caleb. Whether it was for enjoyment or for his lusts for pain and suffering, Onyx was always his favorite to manipulate and play with. Onyx went into the bathroom and grabbed a washcloth from the silver towel rack.

The water was still cold but it was good enough. In Onyx's mind, she should not be helping him. She should have just listened to Elliot and snapped his neck. He had no family here and they all had doubts that anyone would come looking for him. In his car there were no types of identification, not even a registration.

Loren suggested burning the car along with him inside, that way it would look like an accident, beside the lack of identification, and no one would investigate an accident. When Onyx placed the wet towel on his forehead, Damien began to stir. But she could not bring herself to think of taking someone else's life. She thought about it once and that turned her last feeding into a murder gone wrong. It gave her nightmares for months.

"What happened?" Damien said as he came to.

"You fell over. Sorry about that." No matter how much Loren and Elliot wanted to kill him, they all agreed that the information that he had locked away was valuable enough to keep him alive for now.

"Where are the others that where with you?"

Onyx looked past him and searched for a better answer. "They left, figured you need room to breathe." But Damien didn't believe her.

"They don't trust me, is that it? I saw the way the blonde kept looking at me, as if I was some main dish, or her favorite dessert."

Onyx shook her head in disagreement: If only you had the slightest idea how close you were to dying tonight. "Can you just leave it alone?" Onyx glared. The more Damien pushed, the angrier she got, the closer to the brink of thirst.

"No, your 'friend' obviously has a problem with me, so she can come tell me herself," he said, pushing himself up from the bed. The pale walls were paper-thin. Not that it mattered, but Elliot and Loren could still hear. Elliot made it very clear that he didn't want Damien within his sight. Delusional yellow rat was the only nice term he could use for Damien and his prying questions.

"Loren doesn't have a problem with you." A glass shattered in the distance. "It's just that you know so much about us and we know nothing about you." Damien flopped down on the bed with no remorse.

"I guess I understand where they are coming from, but I have nothing to hide. My name is Damien Cornelius Pierce. I'm from Ohio. Born—"

"That's not what we meant…your second name is Cornelius." Onyx pondered. "That is beside the point right now. It's not information we want; it's if we can believe you, or trust you for that matter."

Damien placed his hand on top of hers and smiled. "I swear you can trust me. I have nothing to hide. And I have no reason to lie to any of you."

As Onyx walked out of the room, she silently resented the loner. Trust was a narrow bridge for her kind. No one is a sinner, but that doesn't mean heaven will open its gate for them.

"I'll start trusting you when you start telling us the truth."

After a few moments of thought, Onyx went back inside the room to find that Damien was lying on the couch on the opposite side of the bed.

"So are you ready to trust me, or am I just wasting my time?" He said with a smirk. He had heard her.

"It's nothing like that—it's just that you have met Caleb and know who he is. Including the idea that he knows that you are here with us. It does not make us feel at ease about the situation. You understand why it is rather difficult for us to trust you?"

"What is it about this guy that's got all of ya'll paranoid? You act as if he is some kind of monster out for your lives. And what are you, because I really doubt that any of you are human."

"You would probably call us vampires, but we are not. We don't drink blood—at least not all the time, but we do take some of your essence away. Some of us believe that that we are vampires."

"So what do you call yourself? And what is essence?"

"I call us, alma ladrón, or soul stealers. We don't do it to kill, only to survive. It's normal for some of us to drain a human of both blood and essence until the victim is close to death. It's difficult not to go overboard; it heightens our senses as well as sustains our life. Essence is and can be many things: the life, soul, or even the personality of one's being. None of us are really sure, but we all know it's what keeps us alive. But sometimes we do go overboard, which is why many of us fear Caleb. He killed one of us who got too close to exposing our kind; so, Caleb decided to take care of the problem. He felt that he needed to be the judge, jury, and executioner."

"Oh." Damien sighed as he took another swig of his drink. "Damn, so were you close to the guy?"

"We all were." Onyx refilled their drinks and tossed it down her throat. "Loren was his sister. They had a brother—made from the same family— but the other died in a fire. After that, they have not seen eye to eye about anything. Every time they've seen one another, blades and guns have been drawn. Each of them carries a physical and mental scar created by the other; it's hard to trust someone after they have cause so much hardship. A mutual friend of ours would stop the fight before someone was killed.

Elliot and Caleb were close friends and travelling companions. Elliot knows him from a war that they both served in, but Caleb betrayed him, made the party think that he was a traitor to the cause and that he had allied himself to the enemy. Elliot was almost on the firing squad, had it not been for the commander defending him. Elliot has never forgiven him for his treason.

"When the commander found out, they ordered Caleb's surrender and charged him with treason. He was sentence to be hanged, but our friend saved him the night before his execution. He even begged Elliot not to kill Caleb for his betrayal." She swallowed the last bit of her drink and rinsed out the cup.

"You all seemed to be attached to this friend. What was he to you? And how do you know Caleb?"

"I loved him; he was everything to me. And Caleb was my creator."

Damien took a step back and looked dazed. "He created you? How did he…How is that possible?"

"He gave me a piece of his soul. As I have said, we are like vampires but we are not. The only way to turn us into alma ladrón is if we are on the brink of death, and there are certain people who can become like us. It's hard to find someone, but it is not impossible. The moment you are on the brink of your life ending an alma ladrón must willing give you a portion of their soul without damaging themselves as well as you conscious. If there is just a fracture of a mistake made you could destroy the body, mind, soul or the entire being you were trying to save. Only the strongest can perform the

"So how many lives have you had?"

Onyx sighed, but this time Elliot answered as he and Loren walked into the room.

"It's hard to say and even harder to explain. Hell even Plato and Socrates argued over the matter. To humans and their descendants, you'd believe that you were looking at a reincarnation of a past life. We are not aware of different lives nor can we live more than one—it is just not possible. We are merely fragments that never shift nor change during the time. What we do is change our names and move to different locations. Your perspective is rebirth, but to us it's only one being. All we do is change our names, never our faces, but as you humans age you never notice us—not really. Hell, I saw a broad that I meet during Woodstock with her granddaughter and she asked me if I had known someone that looked exactly like me. It was tragic, so I told her I was his great grandson and that he passed away in his sleep. She tried to set me up with her granddaughter afterwards. It was a little weird, but I took it as a compliment."

"That's awful."

Loren snickered and passed another drink to Elliot. "It happens. What do you want us to say? 'Yes, I'm your old lover and I never age.' What do you expect us to do, huh? Tell everyone who or what we are? We risk exposure and when that happens a lot of bad things come to the alma as well as the human that we get entangled with. That's just plain stupid. And would get us all killed. Don't get me wrong we can still fed and use humans for the bare necessities if need be but we tried to have as little communication or contact with humans. It's one of several reasons why we stay to ourselves sometimes. Hell, Caleb tried his damn hardest to keep some of us from the truth, as well as the humans, no matter what it cost us. To be honest I am surprised that Caleb told you secrets but didn't explain the weight of that knowledge-the naïve fool."

"I'm sorry if I pushed too hard." Damien looked down at his drink in disgusted. He knew he had been lied to but the extent of the lie was truthful. All his research, all of his efforts were wasted.

Loren shrugged it off. "No big deal. You're the first human that we've talked to about this. So don't worry about hurting our feelings. That shit passed a long, long time ago. So ask until you are blue in the face."

"Okay. Did you die in any of them? Your lives I mean," Damien said as he took his shot.

"Now that I can answer," Onyx said. "None of us have actually died, not technically." Stop stalling, chica. I think you are starting to confuse him. "See, as I've said, we are on the brink on death before transformation; that is the main difference between us and the myth of vampirism.

"At the brink of death, we are still alive; there is a little faint heartbeat. Our breath is still and jagged barely a sound that can be reached by the ear. Our skin begins to run cold almost ice against the wind during a snow storm. At that moment everything around you slows down and you feel like everything the smallest detail of your human life was meaningless.

And in that moment we are given the extra soul, or anima as we call it, we become whole again, but we become shadows, and we do whatever we can to survive. The body is still weak after the transformation so we as alma ladrón have two options: we can steal a partial soul of a human and let it manifest into the body until we feel some human senses or emotions.

The second option is drinking and draining either a human or another ladrón dry, but hardly anybody I have heard of has tried and succeed. Most who attempt end up going mad or killing themselves in the process. The body is not strong enough to drain blood from any creature of the earth.

"That is a little bit clearer. So you are not reincarnations. You are like vampires, but I'm guessing if vampires existed they would not stand a chance against you guys. Kind of heavy, but I'm starting to understand now, but what is it like to be someone else? To live in every century and live through it all—hell, you probably saw Jesus Christ himself."

All of a sudden, the three of them burst into laughter. "What, what did I say?" Elliot tried to speak.

"Don't take it personally, but it's an inside joke. We don't really know who the original alma ladrón is and we don't care, but it does cross our minds once or twice a decade or so. Hence the laughter."

"So what does Caleb want?" Then the laughter stopped.

"What I want is for you to get away from what is mine."

As they looked up, they saw Caleb sitting in a against a bartop.

Chapter Nine

Clashing Winds

Caleb jumped down from the tree and his movements became less of a man, lazy and clumsy, and more of a hunter. The predator he had always hidden from everyone else. The stalk in his walk began to shift into the graceful but deadly stride of an animal looking for its next meal. "It's truly sad. I made you come here to bring her back to me, and instead you grow sympathy for these simpletons."

"You lied to me, Benjamin, or Caleb, whatever your name is. You have been lying all this time. You killed someone. You never told me that—"

Silence! As his irises began to glow, Caleb pushed the thought inside of his mind. Damien remained motionless and quiet.

"What did you do to him?" Onyx said as she tried to grab Damien's arm, but he would not budge.

"Making him do what he should have done in the first place, kill you." The voice rang into everyone's mind-only Damien was effected.

Loren tried to lead Onyx away from the intruder but Damien grabbed Loren by the shoulders and slid her into the wall. He grabbed Onyx by her throat and slammed her into the wall. Elliot was not able to help for he was busy trying to throw Caleb out of the nearby window. But to no avail.

"Give up brother, I don't have time to test strength against you not do I want to catch up on old times." Caleb pushed Elliot against the back wall dismantling the beam of the foundation. "I have waited to see you at my mercy and to think a human got the better of you, dear little pet."

Loren slammed against Damien loosening his grip on her friend.

"Get out of here Onyx, you are what they are after." Without hesitation she bolted for the door and didn't look back.

Onyx began to run out of the parking lot into the woods behind the bar. She tried to sense if anyone had been behind her. She knew that Loren and Elliot would not be able to follow as they dealt with both Damien as well as Caleb. She tried to be cautious be her body began to slow and give out.

She was getting tired of running away, but she needed help. As she made her way into the clearing of the forest she noticed a scorch mark that lead towards a trail. The trail ended with a pile of lumber and burnt materials that surrounded the closing area. She wanted to stop and inspect it but she began to sense someone close. Before she passed the smoldering wood something blinded her as she pasted it. Stopping to a screeching halt she saw the figure in the clearing.

Damien stood at the top of the tree and stared down at her. What are you? He pulled a sheath from behind his back and jumped down to charge at her. Before he could strike, she broke a piece of bark off of the nearest tree and used it as a shield. Damien, why are you doing this? Snap out of it. His eyes did not blind in response.

"He can't hear you, sweetheart. He is under my control. Loren has the ability to read the minds, memories, and essences of soul stealers. Elliot has strength that can rival any man, and can alter the thoughts of our kind and humans as well. And you, my dear, your power is something that I thought I'd never see."

Onyx tried to dodge Damien's attacks, but Caleb came out of nowhere and slammed her against a tree. Damien stood there in confusion as he watched his master torture his friend, but he did nothing to stop it. He was completely powerless.

'Come Damien your friend would love a demonstration of the pain you can inflict. Join me.' Caleb bit down on her shoulder blade and tore at the skin. He was letting her feel every bit of pain that was possible. Damien came from behind and began to take stabs at her skin. She screamed, as the pain would not stop. "Let go of me, both of you." Onyx slammed her foot into Caleb's torso and punched Damien so hard in the jaw he crashed into the tree trunk. Caleb stood up and grabbed Onyx by the throat and lifted her off her feet. As she gasped for air, Damien took a hidden blade out and began to press it against the opposite shoulder blade. A tear slide down Damien's cheek.

"You always try to defy me, and you never learn, do you," he yelled as he threw her into the tree and tossed her into the nearby stream. Onyx wobbled to her feet as Caleb quickly sprinted to her side. Onyx tried to defend herself once more, but she was in so much pain that she could barely lift her finger, let alone throw a punch. He tossed her on the ground and bit down into her flesh once more, but before he could finish, Damien cut in between them.

"What are you doing? Either you help me kill her or you stay out of my way, do you understand," Damien did not answer him. "Fine, I will let you finish her off, go ahead and kill her." Nothing. Damien did not even a flinch. His eyes stood still.

"What the hell is the matter with you, Damien? I said kill her now." But Damien did not move. He just stood there and Loren stepped out of the darkness. As Loren moved closer to the light Caleb notice that she was flexing her fingers in the most unusual way. Onyx began to chuckle.

"Sad, isn't big brother, to have someone control your puppet better than you ever could. Turns out I can manipulate others, not only the essences of humans. I figured out that Damien is one of us the moment he went to his car. That's the reason why I was booted out of his mind at first, because he is one of us. The poor thing is so novice that he does not even know that he is an alma ladrón. Which would explain the burning fleshing that I smelled a few minutes ago when I entered the forest. His body has not completely gone through the change but he is still one of us; his body is just too weak to complete the transformation. Am I right? I never pegged you for trying to master that ability: to create. Especially after your last screw up with Jack the Ripper.But this one is-this little kid almost had me fool. But you messed up, because he was just too green, too new-that you could smell death on him. But he is no human that is for damn sure.

"No human could resist trying to figure out what we are. And he asked all the right questions, not as though he was trained, as if he already knew the answers," she said, and as she raised her arms, Caleb began to do the same thing. "I can also control ladrónes de alma as well." She gestured to Caleb to take the blade from Damien, but before she could make him commit suicide, she made him stop.

"Oh, dear sister, Damien is unfortunately human. He's just another pawn in Caleb's game to capture us." Elliot came out of the clearing and just stood there. But his features had changed. The olive color blended into light copper skin tone. His eye began to tarnish into brownish-yellow eyes that would always become shrouded against his black hair. "I thought you would want to see our brother one last time," Loren said as she moved toward Onyx.

Onyx gasped and broke down in tears. After one look in Elliot's direction she began to break down. Thoughts began to ring inside her head. His death. Her betrayal. How was this even possible? Her love was still alive.

"Jarieck, but I saw you die."

"So, big brother, you still live," Caleb said as he tried to drop the blade, but then Loren raised her hand to her back, making Caleb mimic the same gesture and movement with his own body. Caleb pulled out his slender blade and began to aim it towards his very chest.

"Don't worry, Loren, I'm not here to interrupt, nor do I wish to intervene. I'm here to watch, but while I'm at it, Caleb why don't you be a gent, and tell Onyx what you told me in 1869."

"Go to hell, you maggot." Damien answered for his master. Loren's control had broken for a moment giving Damien an opening to attack Jarieck, but it was to no avail. Jarieck took Damien by the neck and snapped it. The boy was dead and gone were his ties to Caleb, who still felt the damage since he could not and had not released his hold on Damien.

"Sorry, but I was in hell. Pretending for centuries that I was someone I was not. And right now, I kind of enjoy the idea of knowing that I get to watch you die today, right in front of our family's eyes. So, Loren, if you would do the honors." Caleb tried once more to get free, but it was useless. He was trapped and the family he once betrayed would see to his death. "Still plan on keeping your secret?"

"I don't know what you are babbling about. I have no secrets brother...you know that."

"You killed the royal and tried to frame me. You slipped me poison and made Amelia watch me die. You should be lucky it's not my hand that wants you dead, but your own. If Loren did not have you by the blade I'd see it twisted against your spine by my own hands. For your sins and your faults, may you feel as much of the pain as you have given others, both essences of humans and ladrónes de alma."

Loren placed her fists closed to her chest as Caleb mimicked every movement pushing the blades close to his heart. As Loren held her breath for a moment she watched Caleb mimic her to the very end as he slowly began to twist the blade into his very heart. Caleb struggled to stop himself from completing the deed, but Loren's pull over his body and mind was stronger than his.

"Or would you like to do the honors, Onyx?" Loren paused as Jarieck walked toward her. Onyx stared into Caleb's eyes and began to feel sorry for him. But her memories came back to her. The fires he started in Rome to smoke her out. The spilled blood from the villages to Cairo to the city of Alexander the Great, only to learn if her scent was still there. He followed her and killed so many to make her existence miserable. And it was finally over—she was free.

"No. Loren, you do the honors. He deserves to fall by his own hand." And with that, Loren twisted her right hand into a fist and slowly pushed it into her chest. Caleb mimicked the move and gritted his canines in pain. Loren did the same gesture, but slowly pulled her closed hand from her chest and slammed it into her back. Caleb cried out in pain. As he fell to the ground, they all saw him rise as the angel that they all loved and respected, but then descend as the demon that Caleb once was.

"He was our brother, but something had to be done about him. Now he can rest in peace."

"It's better this way," Loren said as she lit a match.

I will always love each and every one of you…see you soon.

Epilogue

After the Rain

"I can't believe he's dead. I mean I feel as though I'll miss him, but I can't help but wonder, why try to put us all through such misery, especially you? Damn, and Loren, the nightmares he caused her since my supposed death. My brother was chaotic to the very end. But still even then in the bitter end— he refused to confess his sins. It almost makes you wonder if he had any faults or sins at all." Jarieck said as he walked into the meadow with Onyx. They decided to leave the city and go take a vacation in the woods. Alex and Jena had no problem with that after all three of them had been fired for some unknown reason.

"What do you mean," Onyx said as she stopped.

"He was lying, right?"

"That's what I thought, but in my memories Caleb was with me when the royal was murdered. But..." Elliot said as he stared into her eyes.

"What's wrong?"

"I don't remember seeing you—" Before he could finish, Onyx stabbed him with a double edge. "I'm sorry, love, but here's the thing: I was raped by that royal prick, or at least he tried and I wanted my revenge. He tried to leave me for dead in some Godforsaken back alley. Can you image the sight of it all when I came to? That night while you and Caleb decided to celebrate, I followed him to the taverns, and took my revenge. You could only imagine what pain I put him through after he saw me still alive. It was not a pretty sight mind you. I would have been able to kill him the night he beat and raped me, but I had not fed so he overpowered me. So I drained him bone-dry; it was the least I could do. You and Caleb did teach me: Do on to others what they do to me… Am I right? I was not satisfied with leaving him there though. A man found dead in a brothel is nothing to yawn at. So, I mutilated him and left him outside his bride-to-be's cottage. Or at least I was going to. If only Caleb would have stayed out it, he could have lived. Spouting all that high and mighty righteousness -over- vengeance bull. Ugh all that none sense gave me a headache. And I didn't want you to know either… The thought of you hating me—I just could not bear that feeling."

"Caleb and I could have helped you," he said and coughed.

"You two were busy, but Caleb did catch me when I was on the brink of killing him, but I destroyed his memories and made him think you did it. That was my mistake, but after you died, his memory came back, and he has been trying to kill me ever since. 'Treason' was what he said I had committed, and that I should pay for my crime. I'll give him this; he was loyal to the end. Bitter end, the bitter man, wouldn't you say? But I will say this much, his devotion to you was admirable. Maybe I should show you what really happened." And with that, she placed her cold lips against his warm mouth, slithering into his memory, showing him that horrid night.

"Brother, I think you should stop before Amelia and I have to pick your carcass off the pavement." Benjamin laughed as the barmaid handed them both another pitcher. Jarieck rolled his eyes at his brother, muttering something about a cat. While the two of you were in your merriment, I was upstairs screaming and crying for my life.

"Please, sir, you are a married man," Amelia cried as he ripped at her corset.

"Not till the morrow, love. Now show me why I should leave the countess for your loveliness. Your skin is so much fairer than hers, and you smell twice as good." I tried to fight back, but in my weakened state, I was unable to defend myself against him.

"I said STOP, you bastard." The royal slapped Amelia to the bed. He pulled out his short blade and pressed it against her collarbone.

"And I told you to shut your bloody mouth, you fucking wench."

Finally, my hungry took over and saved me. My body started to shuttered and before I knew it I just stopped moving. I could not fight him in that stage.

"That's right, do what I say and I'll give you a beautiful present to go with your skin." He laughed as he slobbered on her neck. "Maybe an emerald to match your eyes." In an instance I was the dominate predator again. I straddled him and stared down at my prey.

"I'm sorry, were you trying to rape me. And you call yourself a gentleman; I should have your tongue for such a tale." I gave him a lasting kiss that his little bride could and would never give him. And as I kissed him I forced him to submit to me. Opened his mouth as my tongued danced with his and ripped the prick's tongue clean out of his throat. You should have seen him gurgling that pitiful scream. "Yum." After having my fill out blood and his tongue I took my nail and slit his throat.

"Amelia."

But alas that's when Benjamin caught me in the act.

"What have you done? You're going to kill him."

"Really?" She turned to the royal and played with his face. "I thought I was just having fun with him. After all, he's getting married tomorrow, Benjamin." She laughed as she slid off the bed.

"You're going to kill him."

"He was trying to rape me, Benjamin! What was I supposed to do? I was scared and he wouldn't stop. And I was just so hungry; his anger and rage were getting to me and I just lost myself. Please don't tell Jarieck. He would never forgive me." Amelia began to cry.

I really think that Benjamin felt sorry for me. I mean I was helpless.

"Amelia, we have to tell him. We can say that he forced himself on you and that—"

"SHUT up! Do you know how you sound? Just forget what you saw. Go away, I'll clean it up myself."

And that's what he did. He walked out like nothing happened, and when you found the body you must have lost control and nearly killed him, because I heard you and Benjamin fighting. I never thought you two would go so far as to try and kill each other.

"Just do it already." Benjamin paced back and forth and stomped with every turn he made.

His newfound memories wanted me to kill you, but I felt too guilty. I didn't know how to get the other memories back, and your time was ticking away.

"What do you expect me to do, Benjamin, let him die here and walk away?"

He stopped and looked to see if anyone was around. The town was silent, and at a quarter past one, the only thing that broke the silence was the father clock that faced the middle of the town. The shutters of every house were either closed or the candle that was once burning in them was blown out. Silence was easy, so was hiding a body, but they could not leave him. Not their travelling companion and closest friend.

At least she could not leave him. "Of course not, Amelia, but we have to stop the bleeding. And we can't take the soul or the blood out without causing more pain." All of a sudden, the young man screamed out in pain. Blood seeped out of every hole on his face.

"Jarieck, please hold on," Amelia said as she pulled his head into her lap and began to sing to calm him down:

I don't know if you can see,

The changes that have come over me

In these last few days,

I've been afraid

that I might drift away…

Jarieck—even with his face full of blood—was beautiful. He had a light copper skin tone with brownish-yellow eyes that were concealed by his black hair. His black petticoat and white slacks were soiled with blood and tears.

"Lady Amelia, Brother Benjamin, please leave me. They will find the body and go to our inn. You must go," Jarieck said, coughing and hacking every word.

"We are not leaving you. Please don't do this," Amelia cried as she tried to constrict and bind the soul. The deceitful ingrate that tampered with the soul was experienced and knew exactly how to kill them, but Amelia knew how to counter it.

"What? Amelia, what are you doing," Jarieck and Benjamin questioned deeply. "You'll kill us both, darling."

"I don't care," she screamed. "This is all my fault. You can't leave us. You promised us, and you promised me. So please don't die. I'm so sorry. I'll do whatever it takes to keep you alive." Before she could finish, Benjamin tore her away from Jarieck.

"You impudent fool. Let go of me, we have to save him."

Benjamin pushed her into the street. "He made his choice. We warned him to stop making trouble and what does he do? Start a fight in a brothel and then find a royal son close to his engagement and decides to try and drain him dry. He had to be stopped, Amelia."

"What do you mean, he had to be stopped? What did you—" She stopped as she saw that Jarieck had died with no one at his side.

"I'm so sorry, my love. For not telling you, Amelia, I love you and I want you to stay by Benjamin's side as if I never left. I will see you again."

"You, you killed him, didn't you. How could you? He was your best friend."

"Yes, the best friend of mine that was not only betraying me by being with you but also feeding from you, Amelia. You were not supposed to lie with him. He was using your sympathy for him to convince you to let him feed," Benjamin said as he pushed her away from the body.

"So, where is the body he drained?"

"In the river—so drunk he accidently fell into the Hudson River. Tragic, really, and on the eve of his wedding. Such a shame to leave such a beautiful bride at the alter to mourn so young."

Amelia slammed Benjamin into the wall and torn at his flesh. "Temper, temper, remember what you promised your lover."

"That was before you left him to die. Why? Why did you kill Jarieck, your only friend?"

"Because he loved you, and you were mine first." Benjamin flashed into her mind the night that they lay together and gave blood to one another. Before Jarieck had arrived in London and before she was even old enough to understand their bond.

"That was to keep you alive, you had not eaten in days, Benjamin. I was trying to save your life."

"And the kiss, the fact that within that moment I gave you what no other man could give you in your former life."

"Go to hell. I never want to see your face and I never want to know that you exist. Good bye, Benjamin, I hope you enjoy your existence alone."

And I guess after that Benjamin snapped out of it and began to remember.

"It's funny you should say that," Benjamin said as he reappeared in front of Amelia. "Because the existence of what really happened came back when my brother died." He slammed Amelia against the brick wall. "We could have helped you. And you pitted us against one another."

"I was not trying, I swear. I don't even know what happened. I didn't know I had that power. I swear. I'm so sorry Benjamin, truly I am."

"Do you think that's going to bring him back, huh, because it won't?"

Before Benjamin could get his hands on me again, a guard came to investigate the noise and I ran off, and I've been running since.

If I should become a stranger

You know that it would make me

More than sad

Caledonia's been everything

I've ever had

"Loren." Jarieck choked out bits of blood.

"She knew, because I told her the same night I got away from Caleb, and being as your sister was raped and murdered before she came to this life, she understood what I was going through. She pitied me and thought that Caleb was too rash, and that it was because my abilities developed before any of us could realize. So she helped me and manipulated him to get drunk and drown himself by wafting into the deepest part of the bay."

"The orchid and the lily." Jarieck sighed as he gave his final laugh. "Caleb always thought those names were perfect for the two of you. Bittersweet smells, yet so beautiful to look at. You both—"

The knife went deeper.

"Yes, we killed you, Caleb, and the essence to cover our tracks, but I really didn't want to kill you. Because I do and always will love you, Jeremiah, Jarieck, Emmanuel, Elliot. Every life you have had I remember and love. I will see you again," Onyx said as a tear slid down her cheek.

"You will love it in hell, where the both of you belong," Jarieck said as he fell into the wildflowers. Onyx could not help but cry.

Is the deed done, sister? Loren whispered into Onyx's mind.

Yes, she answered, trying not to cry for her lost love. He would never forgive them. Neither would Caleb. There was nothing they could have done to fix their mistakes.

Then I will meet you at the tower at midnight to burn the body. Loren was not happy to see either one of her brothers go, but Onyx needed to be set free. Caleb would have kept hunting her and Jarieck would have probably started helping once he knew the truth. They both had to die. Onyx, I'm sorry.

There was no answer or word back. Onyx.

Onyx left the meadow with Jarieck's body; the dead weight alone was too much to bear. She could feel him slipping away from this world, from her, but she refused to lose him. Outside of the entrance, she found her car still park and still warm. She laid Jarieck in the back seat and started the car. Onyx refused to burn his body, not when there was a chance to save him. When he could be with her again.

She made it to the apartment and tried to bring an essence to her. When he was brought back he would need to be fed, and soon. Loren was right in front of the door and had seen the car pull in front of the parking lot of the motel.

"What are you doing? What about what we discussed? Have you lost your mind or thought of what he will do once you bring him back?"

"Please, Loren. He is your brother and I love him. Please." Loren pulled off her jacket and snatched a soul that was leaving the world. She concentrated and pushed the essence back into the lifeless body.

"My sisters…"

To Be Continued…

Tyesha J'Nae Franklin is a freelance writer for Lake Charles, Louisiana. She mainly writes and focuses on fiction and creative nonfiction works. Even though, Tyesha is a novice writer she is determined to see her novels on the shelf. She is on a break from pursuing her degree towards Creative Writing, Professional Writing, and Psychology, while raising her three children. She is a huge fan of Pokémon. When she is not focused on her laptop screen or her tablet, she spends her free time learning Spanish, taking care of her three children as well as her four dogs and cat. You can reach her at tj_angel_jnae@live.com or on Twitter @JnaeTj.